To Clark and Faye, who make storytelling so much fun.

To the Alaska Raptor Center and their family of raptors, for my inspiration.

Copyright © 2018 by R. D. Sullivan

ISBN: 978-0-9977969-3-3

Tulu Goes Home

by R. D. Sullivan

Today I am finally leaving the Raptor Center.
I can see my big green forest from here.

READY…   SET…

JUMP!

I will circle back around before I say goodbye.
After all, they fixed my broken wing so I could fly.

It's getting darker.
The moonlight will make it a cinch to spot my mouse.
I'll just sit and wait.

Hmmm — I'm still waiting ... no mouse yet.
Mouse hunting is harder
than I remember.

"That's good, Tulu.
But your outdoorsy skills
are a little rusty.
You didn't hear me behind you.
I felt like pecking your head,
but I tooted you instead."

"Quick... get it, Tulu!"

"Where are we, Petey?
You took me to a ... BIRD forest."

"It's a secret woodpecker forest.
Pick out a good spot, Tulu."

"This one is way too big.
Anything could get in here."

"This one feels way too small.
Am I sticking out?"

"Do you see him?
He's on top of that tree
— waiting to eat us both."

"That's my friend from the Raptor Center!
Watch this, Petey."

I am not going to watch.
This can't be good.

"I almost caught a grasshopper. But I haven't seen a single yummy mouse yet!"

"Fish are yummier. However, if I were in a mouse mood ... I'd get down low with the critters."

"That's exactly what my friend said."

THE
END

Rita Sullivan has raised her family in Southern California and lives with her husband and their Boston Terrier, Hanna. Rita's inspiration for writing this book came from her amazing visit to Alaska, where she left her heart somewhere between a dog sled ride on Mendenhall Glacier and the Alaska Raptor Center in Sitka. Since her visit, she has adopted several Alaskan eagles and owls who are most likely soaring somewhere in their big, green forest!

Rich Olson loves dogs, drawing and fixing old historical houses. He also loves to illustrate picture books – especially when cute, fuzzy, furry animals are involved. He grew up in California but he loves the midwest, even with its tornados and torrential downpours. If you would like to say hello, you can email Rich at braintofu@gmail.com.

CPSIA information can be obtained
at www.ICGtesting.com
Printed in the USA
BVHW022229010619
549856BV00002B/2/P

9 780997 796933